W9-BZC-209

KLOOZ

The Puzzle of the Power Drain

by J. Banscherus

translated by Daniel C. Baron

illustrated by Ralf Butschkow

Librarian Reviewer
Marci Peschke
Librarian, Dallas Independent School District
MA Education Reading Specialist, Stephen F. Austin State University
Learning Resources Endorsement, Texas Women's University

Reading Consultant
Sherry Klehr
Elementary/Middle School Educator, Edina Public Schools, MN
MA in Education, University of Minnesota

STONE ARCH BOOKS
Minneapolis   San Diego

First published in the United States in 2008
by Stone Arch Books
151 Good Counsel Drive, P.O. Box 669
Mankato, Minnesota 56002
www.stonearchbooks.com

First published by Arena Books
Rottendorfer str. 16, D-97074
Würzburg, Germany

Library of Congress Cataloging-in-Publication Data
Banscherus, Jürgen.
[Dad blaue Karussell. English.]
The Puzzle of the Power Drain / by J. Banscherus; translated by
Daniel C. Baron; illustrated by Ralf Butschkow.
p. cm. — (Klooz)
"Pathway Books."
Summary: When the carnival's merry-go-round is repeatedly
sabotaged, the owner asks Klooz to take the case.
ISBN-13: 978-1-59889-876-7 (library binding)
ISBN-10: 1-59889-876-0 (library binding)
ISBN-13: 978-1-59889-912-2 (paperback)
ISBN-10: 1-59889-912-0 (paperback)
[1. Carnivals—Fiction. 2. Mystery and detective stories.] I. Baron,
Daniel C. II. Butschkow, Ralf, ill. III. Title.
PZ7.B22927Pu 2008
[Fic]—dc22   2007006624

Art Director: Heather Kindseth
Graphic Designer: Kay Fraser

1 2 3 4 5 6 12 11 10 09 08 07

Printed in the United States of America

Table of contents

KLOOZ

The Puzzle of the Power Drain

OP SECRET

CHAPTER 1

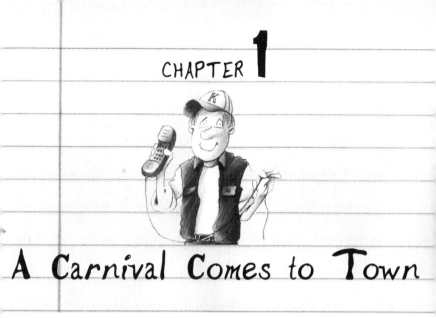

A Carnival Comes to Town

My name is Klooz, and I am a private detective.

Right now, I am lying on my bed. I am listening to music, chewing my wonderful Carpenter's gum, and drinking some cold milk.

For the first time I can remember, I am happy that I don't have a case to work on. The carnival that just ended really wore me out.

Sorry, first things first. My story began a few days before the carnival ended.

The first few days of the carnival I ran home every day after school. I gobbled down my dinner, and then took off full speed to the carnival. My mom only saw the cloud of dust I left behind.

Then one day, I realized that I was completely broke.

I stood in the kitchen. There wasn't anything in my pockets except a penny and a broken key to a bicycle lock.

I had no money left for the carnival.

To make matters worse, my supply of Carpenter's chewing gum was also getting smaller.

Without my Carpenter's gum, I am only half a person.

I had to go get some more. Maybe Olga would let me take some and pay her back later.

Olga owns the newspaper stand that is just around the corner from our apartment. Sometimes she helps me with my cases.

"I would like one pack of Carpenter's gum," I said when I arrived.

"Just one pack?" Olga asked, surprised. "What's wrong, Klooz?"

I reached into my pockets and turned them inside out.

Olga laughed. "You went to the carnival one too many times, right?"

I nodded.

"Could I pay you later?" I asked.

She gave me five packs. "Take them," she said. "You can pay me when you have the money."

Then she reached over the counter to pinch my cheek.

Olga has a big heart and we are good friends, but I don't let anybody pinch my cheeks. Except my mom, every once in a while.

I dodged Olga's hand and was about to go.

Just then, Olga cried, "Wait, Klooz!
You know the blue merry-go-round,
right? The merry-go-round for kids that is
always at the carnival?"

Did I know the merry-go-round? What a dumb question. When I was little, I must have ridden on it at least a hundred times. My mom could barely get me off that thing.

"A while ago, William was here," Olga said. "He owns the merry-go-round."

I unwrapped a stick of chewing gum and put it in my mouth. "So?" I asked.

Olga leaned forward. "He's as mad as can be," she said. She was almost whispering, even though no one was around.

William's merry-go-round was acting strange, Olga told me. It was turning too quickly, or it was stopping in the middle of the ride.

Olga said, "William found little cuts in the power cables that ran the merry-go-round. He is afraid they are going to shut him down because the merry-go-round isn't safe for kids."

"Why doesn't William go to the police?" I wanted to know.

Olga shrugged her shoulders. "He already went to the police. They told him they couldn't send an officer just to watch his merry-go-round."

She paused and looked at me.

Then she said, "What do you think? Could that be a case for you?"

Of course that could be a case for me. Cases without the police are the kind of cases I like.

Olga said, "Find out who is messing with the merry-go-round. Then you don't have to pay me back for that chewing gum I just gave you. Agreed? William is an old friend and I want to help him."

"Did you tell him about me?" I asked.

"I did," Olga replied. "I told him you were the best."

Olga always tells everybody that I am a great detective. That's okay. After all, she is right.

SHERLOCK HOLMES

KLOOZ

Back to the Carnival

I had thought that I was finished with the carnival for this year. Since I was out of money, I didn't think I would be back. Now I was standing in the middle of it. I was as excited as I had been when I rode the roller coaster for the first time this year.

The only difference was that now I didn't have the time or the money for the roller coaster. I had to go to the merry-go-round.

This merry-go-round is smaller than the other rides, but you can't miss it.

That's because of its famous blue top that looks just like a little blue sky.

There aren't any fire trucks, motorcycles, airplanes, or police cars on the blue merry-go-round.

There are just little horses to ride on.

The horses come in all different colors, and each one has a golden saddle and golden mane.

Of course it's all old-fashioned baby stuff, but little kids love it.

Just as I walked up to the ride, the merry-go-round came to a stop.

The parents lifted their kids off the horses.

A girl collected tickets for the next ride. She was about the same age as me and had a braid that reached all the way down her back.

"I am looking for Mr. William," I said to the girl.

She pushed me aside to help a little boy onto a horse.

"What do you want with my uncle?" she asked me over her shoulder.

I leaned against a colorful post that supported the top of the merry-go-round.

"Is it true that there is something wrong with the merry-go-round?" I asked.

The girl looked surprised. She raised her eyebrows. "Who says that?" she asked me.

"I don't know," I said.

Just then, a man wearing a blue hat came out of the ticket booth.

He pressed a button and the horses on the merry-go-round slowly started to move.

"Hey Uncle William, come here," the girl said.

"What's up, Suzanne?" Uncle William said.

Suzanne pointed at me. "This guy wants to talk to you. It has something to do with the wrecked cables," she told him.

William took a big, flowery handkerchief out of his pocket and wiped the sweat from his forehead.

Then he looked closely at me and asked, "Do you know who has been fooling around with my power cables? Well? If you know who is doing this, you better tell me right away. That is a dirty trick."

Suzanne broke in. "Don't get all upset again, Uncle William!"

William took a deep breath. Then he spoke to me in his normal voice.

"Just who are you, anyway?" he asked.

"I'm a friend of Olga's," I answered. "My name is Klooz, and I am a private detective."

I had hardly gotten those words out of my mouth before William broke out laughing. He laughed so hard he nearly choked.

"I thought . . . I thought . . . ," he finally said. "I thought you were a real detective. Olga told me, 'Klooz will help you. He is the best private detective in the whole city.'"

He started to laugh again. "So Olga sent me a kid!"

The guy was having fun at my expense.

I didn't like that one bit.

"Fine," I said. "Let's see how well you solve this case."

I turned and started to walk away.

It seemed like I wouldn't be taking this case after all. Too bad. I would just explain to Olga what had happened.

I had forgotten about Suzanne. She grabbed my arm and wouldn't let me go.

"My uncle doesn't mean it," she said. "Believe me. He's just tired. He didn't sleep well last night."

"I didn't sleep well?" William yelled.

Boy, he was easy to upset.

"I didn't sleep a wink!" William shouted. "I waited all night for the crook to try again. It was pointless!"

The little kids on the merry-go-round screamed with joy while their parents yelled at them to hold on tight.

I grinned at Suzanne and put my fingers in my ears.

Suddenly, the merry-go-round started to turn more quickly.

The little horses were going up and down like wild mustangs.

At first the kids loved it.

Then the horses sped up more, and the kids started to realize that it wasn't fun and games anymore. Their faces looked terrified. A couple of them looked like they were going to cry, and one girl screamed.

All of the kids held onto their horses as hard as they could. Otherwise, they would have bounced off.

I wouldn't have believed what happened next if I hadn't seen it myself.

With a mighty leap, William jumped over to the controls.

He stopped the ride.

The horses went up and down wildly just a few more times. Then they started to slow down.

Finally, the merry-go-round stopped. Up until then most of the parents had stood there looking scared. Only now did they start to move.

They tore their scared children from the horses. Then they all ran over to William.

The crowd of parents made an angry circle around William. All of the parents were yelling at him.

After a while, William calmed the parents down.

He gave everyone their money back. Suddenly, it was still and quiet at the blue merry-go-round.

"It's been like that for three days now," Suzanne said to me.

Her uncle hung a cardboard sign on the ticket booth.

It read, "Temporarily Closed."

Temporarily Closed

Then William crawled through a trap door in the middle of the merry-go-round to get to the motor. After just one minute, he came back.

He went to the ticket booth. He grabbed duct tape and some tools. Then he disappeared into the merry-go-round again.

"They were here again," Suzanne mumbled as she played with her braid.

I thought about the case.

William must have enemies. Why else would someone want to damage the power cables?

When I asked Suzanne, she said, "Enemies? Uncle William? I have no idea."

Suzanne's uncle was finished before I could ask anything else.

Soon, kids were riding on the horses again, like nothing had ever happened.

"What was it this time?" I asked William.

"The usual," he replied. "Somebody was messing with the electric cables."

"But you were here all last night," I said. "Nobody could have gotten at the cables, right?"

"That's true," William replied. "Besides, the trap door to the motor was locked. I also closed up the whole merry-go-round with a cover and locked that too. It was a brand new lock."

He sighed. "What else could I possibly do?" he asked sadly.

"Did you look this morning to see if the cables were okay?" I asked.

William shook his head. "Why? After all, I kept watch the whole night."

I didn't give in. "You didn't fall asleep, not even for a second?"

He laughed. "Maybe I fell asleep for a minute or two," he said. He looked embarrassed.

"Somebody used that minute or two to cut the cables," I said. "Could I have a look at the cables? Who knows. Maybe I can find a clue."

"Be my guest," William said.

It actually sounded like he meant it. Maybe he wasn't a grump after all.

He opened the door to the motor. Then I climbed into the merry-go-round.

There wasn't much light. All I could see was a bunch of cables. They had been fixed with duct tape.

There were no other clues to be found that could help me solve the case.

By the time I got out of the motor compartment, Suzanne was collecting tickets for the next ride.

Meanwhile, William had a visitor. A tall, thin man with a silver briefcase in his hand was talking to him.

"I can offer you eight thousand dollars," I heard the man say. "Okay, even nine thousand dollars."

"It's not for sale," William said.

"Ten thousand dollars," the visitor said. "Cash. That's my last offer."

William shook his head. "Listen, the merry-go-round is not for sale. My grandfather built it. And my father ran it for fifty years."

"You're not getting any younger," the thin man said to William, smiling. "Soon you won't be able to work."

"Ha!" William yelled. "I'll still be here when you're pushing up daisies!"

"There's no reason to be rude!" the man said.

"Me? Rude?" William yelled. "No money can buy the most beautiful children's carnival ride in the whole world. I am not the rude one! You are, and you're a greedy pig!"

William was angry. The other man quickly tucked the briefcase under his arm. Then he ran away, into the crowd.

"You really showed him, Uncle William!" Suzanne said.

William looked upset. He said, "That guy just gets on my nerves. That was the third time he's been here."

The third time?

What if the thin man was the greedy pig causing the problems that the merry-go-round was having?

Maybe he hoped that soon, William would get tired of having to fix the merry-go-round.

Or maybe he thought William wouldn't be able to afford to run it anymore.

William had made fun of me. However, he really wasn't such a bad guy after all.

"If it's okay with you, I would like to stake out the merry-go-round this evening," I said.

William looked confused. "You are still just a kid."

"I have handled many cases," I told him. "Most of them were more dangerous than this one."

William smiled. "Okay. By the way, what is your first name?" he asked. He stuck out his hand to shake mine.

"The name is Klooz. Just Klooz," I replied. "And my work is not for free."

"If you catch the criminal I'll give you ten free rides on the merry-go-round."

I shook my head and grinned.

"No thanks," I said. "I think that's just for the little kids."

"What if you had the merry-go-round all to yourself?" William asked.

"I don't know," I said.

Then William offered, "All to yourself, and at double the regular speed?"

At double the regular speed? It was a deal!

CHAPTER **3**

Plan in Action

The next night was perfect for my plan.

My mom was working late.

She wouldn't be home until after my bedtime. I would leave while she was still out. Then I would get home before she came home from work.

My mom doesn't mind my detective work, as long as I get my homework done.

She thinks school is really important.

After dinner I went to my bedroom. I was ready to get things together for my stakeout.

I packed a big flashlight and two cartons of milk into my backpack.

Then I stuck a pack of Carpenter's gum in my pocket. It was my last pack. I was in big trouble. I hoped I didn't run out of gum on my stakeout. That would be a disaster.

After my mom left, it was time for me to start working on the case of the blue merry-go-round.

I picked up my backpack and hung the apartment key on my neck.

Then I left the apartment.

I tiptoed out of the building.

We have a couple of nosy neighbors. They would love to complain to my mom about my detective work.

Outside it was cool and clear.

The moon looked like a fat pancake hanging over the city.

I was happy that I had put on my thick winter sweater.

Waiting is bad enough. Waiting and freezing would be awful.

When I arrived at the carnival, it was pretty dead. Almost all of the rides and booths had closed down for the night.

I was almost all alone in that dusty place. It was completely dark. I found a good hiding place by the swinging ship ride. From there, I could see everything I needed to see.

At night everything looked a little different than during daylight.

William's merry-go-round looked like a giant black mushroom. The swinging ship looked like some sort of dangerous monster.

When a cat suddenly cried I almost wet my pants.

I pulled my legs into my sweater so that my feet were sticking out.

Then I waited. I chewed gum, counted stars, and waited. I had to force myself to keep my eyes open. I yawned until my jawbone cracked. Then I waited, and waited.

I waited for nothing. Nobody tried to get in William's merry-go-round.

The only living creatures I saw were the men from a security company.

They made their rounds every hour on the hour.

Every time they walked by, I
ducked behind the swinging ship until
I heard their footsteps going away.

Finally, after a long time, I gave
up. I had drunk the two cartons of
milk and chewed all of my sticks of
gum. I hadn't caught anyone.

My watch said it was ten o'clock. I
had to get home before my mom did.

Before I knew it, I was sitting at the
dining room table as my mom walked
in the front door. As usual, I had set
the table and made coffee. My coffee
is the best — that's what my mom
always says. She sat down and gave
me a kiss.

"You look tired," she said.

"You do too," I said.

She poured herself a cup of coffee. "I was on the late shift," she said.

I almost said, "Me too," but then I thought better of it.

"You probably watched TV for too long," my mom added. "Admit it."

I quickly shook my head. "I really didn't, Mom, I swear!"

I have no idea how I made it through school the next day. I was really tired from my late night. I probably fell asleep and took little catnaps every now and then. Luckily, no one noticed. I can sleep with my eyes open. My mom thinks that is great, but my teachers don't.

I hurried home after school. I wanted to stop by the blue merry-go-round a little later.

My mom was taking a nap. So I warmed up some fries and a hamburger from the day before. As usual, I drank a huge glass of milk.

I wrote my mom a note. It said, "I might be back kind of late."

Then I took off.

I passed Olga's newspaper stand. She waved me over.

"William was just here," she told me. She sounded excited. "He told me that he looked over the cables this morning. They had been cut again. What do you think of that?"

First I didn't understand what she was saying. I had only slept for a few minutes at school, after all.

"Ca-ca-cable?" I finally said.

Olga repeated what she had just said.

"That is impossible!" I cried. "I was there the whole evening!"

"Maybe it was ghosts," Olga said as she rolled her eyes.

"Nonsense," I replied. "I'll find out who it was. You'll see."

CHAPTER 4

All Mixed Up

After I left Olga's, it took me a while to collect my thoughts.

William had locked the trap door to the motor.

He covered the whole merry-go-round. Then he locked the cover. I had spent the entire evening waiting. Still, someone had gotten at the cables.

I'd kept my eye on everything like a watchdog.

When I left, there hadn't been anyone around.

It was impossible that anyone had been there.

Darn, this was a difficult case.

I was pretty mixed up by the time I got back to the merry-go-round.

William had visitors again. He was standing at the ticket booth with two men who I hadn't seen before. All three were waving their arms around and interrupting each other's conversation.

I tried to hear what they were saying to each other. I couldn't understand a single one of them through the noise.

"Get lost!" William said suddenly and loudly. "I have work to do."

The men left. They both looked really angry. "There will be consequences for this!" one of them yelled.

"Who was that?" I asked Suzanne. She had been standing next to me and listening during the entire argument.

"That was Mr. Oak and Mr. Meyer," she explained. "The swinging ship belongs to Mr. Oak and the flying chair ride belongs to Mr. Meyer."

"What do they want from your uncle?" I asked.

"It's always the same. They want Uncle William to raise the price of a ride on the merry-go-round, but he won't do it," Suzanne told me.

The merry-go-round slowly turned. William came over to us.

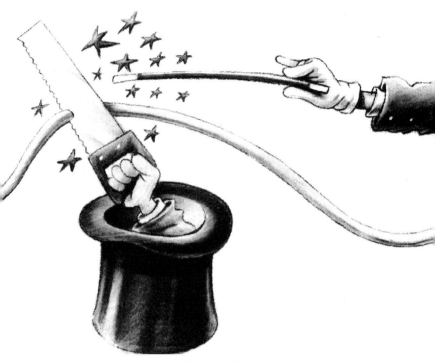

"There must have been magicians here last night, Klooz," he said. "The cables were cut even though you were looking for the crooks. It must be magic."

William made a face. "The lock on the curtain is not at all damaged," he said. "The curtain hasn't been touched either. I might have to shut down the merry-go-round for good."

That would be a disaster!

I knew what he meant. If I were in his shoes, I would be mad too. "I am pretty sure it wasn't magic," I said. "But I didn't see anyone."

One of the men had said, "There'll be consequences for this." What if these men were behind the sabotage? Did the other two men want to get rid of their competition?

I was stuck in a really crazy situation. I had three suspects: the thin man, Mr. Oak, and Mr. Meyer.

However, I didn't have any evidence. Plus, I had no idea how they were committing the crime.

"No one can sit on the cables and watch them," I heard Suzanne tell William.

No one? I thought. Nonsense. Someone could.

That someone was me.

I asked William to give me the key to the merry-go-round until the next day. He wasn't sure at first, but then he agreed.

I would spend another evening at the carnival. If I was unlucky, then nothing would happen.

Maybe I would be lucky.

Maybe, tonight, I would discover what was going on and who was behind it.

To be honest, I was sure that one of the three suspects would show up. Or perhaps someone else. Or perhaps even all three.

When I finally got home, it was early evening. My mom was sitting at the kitchen table drinking coffee. She didn't ask if I had done my homework.

I sat down with her and poured myself a glass of milk.

My mom looked at me. She gave me the look that says, "I know exactly what you are up to."

"Do you have a new case?" she asked.

I nodded.

"Are you going to tell me what it is about?" she asked.

I was too tired to tell her the whole story. So I said, "It's really no big deal, Mom. Nothing exciting."

She brought the dishes to the dishwasher.

"Well, okay," she said. "I feel better already. Could you please do your homework now?"

She remembered after all. I would have been surprised if she had forgotten.

I got a glass of milk from the refrigerator. Then I went into my room and sat down on my bed.

I wanted to relax for a minute before I started my homework.

That evening it took me quite a while to do all my homework, even though I didn't have very much. I couldn't think.

As the night went on, I was becoming more and more nervous. Even my favorite CDs couldn't calm me down.

Finally, I left the house.

I had three packs of Carpenter's gum in my pocket. My favorite gum always helped when I had the jitters.

At the carnival, I hid behind a big trash can until the last people had disappeared.

Then I snuck over to the merry-go-round. I opened the curtain, and locked myself inside.

So that was that.

Nobody would ever guess that I was hidden inside the merry-go-round.

I made myself comfortable between two wood horses. I had brought an old pillow with me so I wouldn't hurt my butt.

Then I waited.

Every hour on the hour I heard the footsteps of the security guards. At some point my feet fell asleep.

I looked at my watch. Only five minutes had passed since the last time I looked at it.

Private detective — what a stupid job! Other boys were at home. They were in their beds, snoring away.

Then I heard something. It rustled, like a piece of paper rubbing against another piece of paper.

I held my breath and listened.

Yes, there it was again. I tried to find out where the noise came from.

I didn't have to search for long. It was coming from the motor. There was no doubt about it.

Somebody was in there. They had gotten past me somehow!

I got shivers down my spine. For a moment, I couldn't think clearly.

Then I said to myself, Klooz, you are a detective. Pull yourself together.

My brain started working again. I had to see who was in there. Right away!

I counted to three. Then I carefully pulled on the door to the motor. I pulled hard, but it didn't move.

The door was locked. Locked! How was that possible? Was it a snake crawling around down there? Or was it a ghost? What if a slimy hand came through the keyhole and tried to grab me? It shook my confidence. However, I knew what I had to do.

With shaking fingers, I stuck the key into the lock and turned it silently. I grabbed my heavy flashlight, ripped the door open, and shined light though the trap door.

CHAPTER 5

Caught the Crooks

The next afternoon, I showed up at the merry-go-round in a great mood. Suzanne and William were shocked.

"Klooz, the cables," William began.

I didn't let him finish. "I have them," I said casually.

"You have who?" William asked.

"Who else?" I said, grinning. "The crooks who have been destroying your cables. I caught them last night."

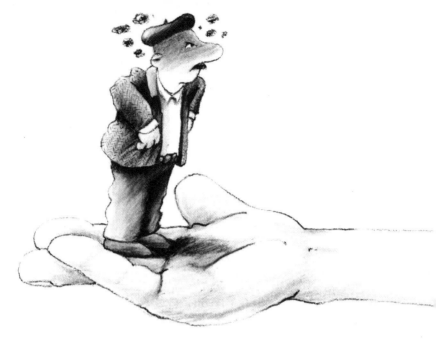

William's face started to turn red.

"Where are they?" he demanded. "Where are those guys? Wait until I get my hands on them. I'll give them a good beating!"

"Take it easy," I said. I tried to calm him down. I took my backpack from my shoulder and placed it on the ground in front of William.

"They are in there," I said.

William looked shocked. "Are you pulling my leg, Klooz? You know the cables were cut again today."

"That was the last time," I said. "You can bet your life on it. So, what do you think? Do you want to know who the criminals are?"

William muttered something that I couldn't hear.

Finally, his curiosity got the better of him. He knelt on the ground, opened the bag, and stuck his nose in it. Then he looked up again. He looked as if he was going to give me a good beating.

"Guinea pigs?" he growled. "It was guinea pigs? I have had enough. If you don't leave immediately . . ."

He was too mad to say anything else. Suzanne grabbed the bag, reached inside and pulled two guinea pigs, one brown and white and the other completely white, into the daylight.

"Gosh, Uncle William," she said excitedly. "That's Nemo and Geraldine!"

Then she turned to me and asked, "How did you ever find them?"

I cleared my throat. "Thanks for finally allowing me to tell you. So, last night I locked myself behind the curtain. Suddenly I heard something rustling in the motor." I paused, to make my story more exciting.

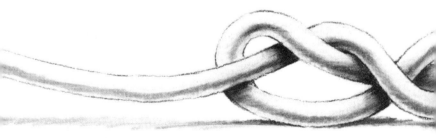

Then I went on, "I looked and found these two down there. They had already gnawed another cable. I put them under my sweater and took them home. That's the whole story."

Of course that wasn't the whole story.

I didn't tell them that I thought the criminal could have been a ghost.

Suzanne hugged the guinea pigs tightly.

"Why didn't we think of that, Uncle William?" she asked.

Then she turned to me and said, "Geraldine and Nemo have run away before. They ate a telephone cord once."

Now William chimed in. "Suzanne brought them here to the carnival to say hello to me. Then they just disappeared."

"I looked for them everywhere," Suzanne added. "Thank you, Klooz."

William looked in the motor compartment. He quickly found the hole that I had found the night before.

"So that's how they were getting in," he said, shaking his head. "Those bratty rats." He offered his hand to me. "Olga was right, Klooz. You really are a great detective."

I shook his hand. "Well," was all I could bring myself to say.

"So how about your free rides?" he asked.

I grinned. "My pay? I'll take that right now!"

William hung a sign on the ticket booth. It read, "Reserved."

I sat down on the biggest horse and it started. Of course it wasn't a roller coaster, but it was fun anyway.

William turned it on full power. On the merry-go-round's fifth time around, he and Suzanne joined me.

* * *

That is my story of the case of the merry-go-round and its puzzling power drain. It's no wonder that now that the carnival is gone, I need rest. Right?

I forgot something important.

Yesterday Olga gave me a pack of gum that was full of holes.

"That is for you," she said. "And this letter came with it."

I unfolded the note and read:

Dear Klooz,

Nemo and Geraldine are doing well. They have recovered from their adventure.

I don't know if I told you that Geraldine just had babies. The baby guinea pigs were happy to get their parents back. Enjoy this pack of gum.

Sincerely,

Suzanne and Uncle William

Now my mom and I have a new roommate. His name is Paul, and he is a baby guinea pig. A wonderful white guinea pig.

The end

About the Author

Jürgen Banscherus is a worldwide phenomenon. There are almost a million Klooz books in print, and they have been translated into Spanish, Danish, Thai, Chinese, and eleven other languages.
He has worked as a newspaper writer, a research scientist, and a teacher. His first book for children was published in 1985. He lives with his family in Germany.

About the Illustrator

Ralf Butschkow was born in Berlin. He works as a freelance graphic designer and illustrator, and has published more than 50 books for children. Critics have praised his work as "thoroughly enjoyable," "creatively original," and "highly recommended."

Glossary

cables (KAY-buhlz)—thick wires

carnival (KAR-nuh-vuhl)—a public celebration, often with rides and games

compartment (kuhm-PART-muhnt)—a separate part of a container

consequences (KON-suh-kwenss-iz)—the results of an action

gnaw (NAW)—to chew on something

guinea pig (GIN-ee PIG)—a small mammal, often kept as a pet

reserved (ri-ZURVD)—kept for someone to use

sabotage (SAB-uh-tahzh)—to damage something on purpose

stakeout (STAYK-owt)—a period of watching for something

suspects (SUHSS-pekts)—people thought to be responsible for a crime

temporarily (tem-por-AIR-uhl-ee)—for a short time

Discussion Questions

1. Klooz has a lot of different suspects while he tries to solve this mystery. Who are they? What were his reasons for suspecting them? How did he finally realize who was to blame?

2. Olga tells Klooz that she wants him to help solve William's case. Have you ever helped a friend by introducing them to someone else? What happened? Talk about it.

3. Have you ever had or known a pet who did something bad? How did you explain what had happened? What did you do about it?

Writing Prompts

1. Do you have a favorite ride at the carnival? Draw a picture of it, and describe how you feel when you are on the ride. Are you scared? Are you excited? Write about it!

2. Geraldine and Nemo are Suzanne's pet guinea pigs. Do you have any pets? Describe your pet, or the pet of someone you know.

3. Sometimes it can be interesting to imagine a story from another character's point of view. Try writing chapter 5 from Suzanne's point of view. What does she see? What does she think about? How does she feel? Write it down!

Internet Sites

Do you want to know more about subjects related to this book? Or are you interested in learning about other topics? Then check out FactHound, a fun, easy way to find Internet sites.

Our investigative staff has already sniffed out great sites for you!

Here's how to use FactHound:

1. Visit *www.facthound.com*

2. Select your grade level.

3. To learn more about subjects related to this book, type in the book's ISBN number: **1598898760**.

4. Click the **Fetch It** button.

FactHound will fetch the best Internet sites for you!